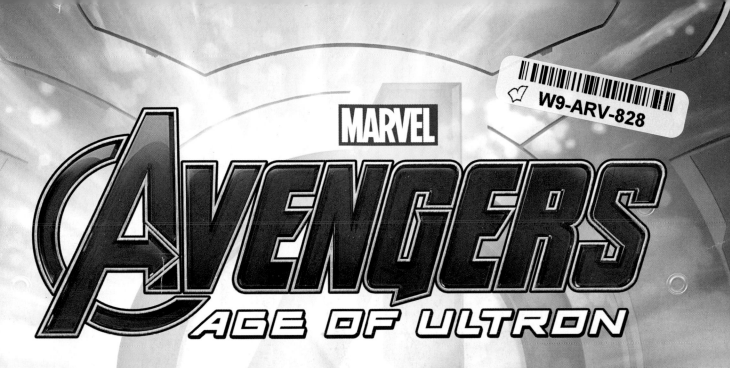

MARVEL

AVENGERS
AGE OF ULTRON

Battle at Avengers Tower

Adaptation by Adam Davis

Illustrated by Ron Lim, Andy Smith, and Andy Troy

Based on the Screenplay by Joss Whedon

Produced by Kevin Feige, p.g.a.

Directed by Joss Whedon

LITTLE, BROWN AND COMPANY
New York Boston

Little, Brown and Company

Hachette Book Group
1290 Avenue of the Americas, New York, NY 10104
Visit us at lb-kids.com

Little, Brown and Company is a division of Hachette Book Group, Inc.
The Little, Brown name and logo are trademarks of Hachette Book Group, Inc.

The publisher is not responsible for websites (or their content) that are not owned by the publisher.

First Edition: April 2015

Library of Congress Control Number: 2014956324

ISBN 978-0-316-25643-8

10 9 8 7 6 5 4 3 2

CW

PRINTED IN THE UNITED STATES OF AMERICA

The Avengers are at war. They are traveling around the world, destroying the remaining clusters of the evil organization known as Hydra. The last base is in Sokovia, and it is the most heavily guarded of them all. The Avengers must fight harder than ever before.

Inside the base, Baron Strucker wants to make sure that Hydra exists far into the future. Through experiments on two willing test subjects, he is close to making that a reality. Pietro and Wanda have super powers and don't like the Avengers.

Meanwhile, in a nearby town, Tony Stark's latest creations, the Iron Legion, ensure peace and order. But the locals do not feel safe. Different groups have been trying to take over for centuries, so the people trust no one—not even the Avengers!

As Captain America, Thor, Black Widow, Hawkeye, and the Hulk fight the Hydra troops, Iron Man works to disable the blue energy around the base. He shoots a digger missile into the ground, taking down the force field for good!

Now inside, Tony Stark looks for the source that is powering the massive structure. Some of the Hydra troops have suits that are powered by the same blue energy. Tony knows he has seen it somewhere before.

While the other Avengers fight off the last of the soldiers outside, Captain America locates Strucker. He throws a grenade at the hero and tries to escape, but Cap swats the grenade out a window with his shield and then knocks Strucker's lights out!

Elsewhere, Tony finds the energy source— Loki's scepter! Loki is Thor's evil brother, and his staff has the ability to control minds and lead alien armies. In the wrong hands, it could cause cities to crumble! Tony takes it carefully, knowing it will be safe at Avengers Tower.

With Loki's scepter in the Avengers' possession and Hydra defeated for good, the team flies the Quinjet back to Avengers Tower. They are triumphant, but they are worried.

The team secures the scepter in Tony's lab. It will be protected by the Iron Legion until Thor can take it back to his home world of Asgard.

Maria Hill, an employee of Stark Industries, briefs Steve Rogers—Captain America—on Pietro and Wanda. Their powers are impressive and dangerous. Pietro can run faster than anyone, and Wanda has the ability to manipulate minds. They volunteered for Strucker's experiments so they could protect their home and fight the Avengers. Steve doesn't like the sound of this.

AMERICA OUT OF SOKOVIA!

NO JUSTICE NO PEACE!

As Jarvis fixes some of the Iron Legionnaires that have been damaged in Sokovia, Bruce Banner—the Hulk's mild-mannered alter ego—and Tony inspect Loki's scepter. "This could be the key to creating Ultron," Tony says. Ultron is something the two scientists have talked about before—a defense system that could protect the whole world.

If Ultron works, the world won't need the Avengers to protect it anymore. Steve doesn't know how he can trust an unthinking, unfeeling computer. Tony is not sure whether the program will work, but he has to try.

Later that night, a party to celebrate Hydra's defeat is in full swing. Tony, Steve, Bruce, and Thor—along with Natasha Romanoff aka Black Widow and Clint Barton aka Hawkeye—laugh and eat good food. It is nice to relax with friends!

Down in Tony's workshop, Loki's scepter pulses with evil energy. Suddenly, Ultron comes to life! The world-protecting system is now something sinister. Ultron has thoughts of his own and wants to escape the confines of the computer. He needs a body so he can be free, though. And Ultron knows exactly how he can escape.

As the party roars on, the Avengers decide to play a game with Thor's hammer. Each member of the team tries to lift it, but only Steve is able to succeed—just barely. Relieved, Thor laughs.

Suddenly, there's a screech! The heroes look over to see one of the broken Iron Legionnaire suits. Ultron has found himself a body! The being says that the Avengers cause more harm than good with their fighting.

Before the Avengers can react, the Iron Legion burst into the room! They are being controlled by Ultron! The heroes don't have time to suit up, so they have to improvise and use the weapons they have at hand.

Bruce transforms into the Hulk and smashes a Legionnaire! Black Widow and Hawkeye strike and dodge the metallic attackers. Cap blocks punches with his shield. Thor summons lightning and fries the circuits of some robots, and Tony shoots repulsor blasts from his gauntlets!

After the Iron Legion is defeated, the Avengers turn to Ultron. They want to know why he is attacking them. "I know you mean well, but there's only one path to peace... human extinction," Ultron explains. Thor is angered and suddenly throws his hammer, smashing Ultron to pieces. As the light in Ultron's eyes dims, he makes one last declaration: "I'm free now."

Across the globe, half-completed robotics come to life and begin creating a new body for Ultron. As he is being built, Ultron smiles, feeling the power his stronger body gives him.

With the help of Maria Hill, the Avengers are able to locate the threat. Ultron is building an army of Sentries that look like him. Ultron knows he will be unstoppable.

The Super Heroes gear up for their toughest battle yet. But no matter what odds they face, they will work as a team and succeed because of it. After all, they are the Avengers!